Someplace Else

Someplace Else

By Carol P. Saul

Illustrated by Barry Root

Simon & Schuster Books for Young Readers

SIMON & SCHUSTER BOOKS FOR YOUNG READERS
An imprint of Simon & Schuster Children's Publishing Division
1230 Avenue of the Americas, New York, NY 10020
Book design by Paul Zakris. The text of this book is set in 14 1/2 Garamond.
The illustrations were done in watercolor.
Manufactured in the United States of America.
10 9 8 7 6 5 4 3 2 1

Library of Congress Cataloging-in-Publication Data
Saul, Carol P.
Someplace else / by Carol P. Saul ; illustrated by Barrett Root.
p. cm.
Summary: When she tires of living in her white house in the orchard,
Mrs. Tillby sets out to find a different place to call home.
[1. Dwellings—Fiction. 2. Voyages and travels—Fiction.]
I. Root, Barry, ill. II. Title.
PZ7.S2504So 1995 [E]—dc20 93-18681
ISBN: 0-689-80273-0

For my mother
—C. P. S.

For Frances Dobbs
—B. R.

All her life Mrs. Tillby had lived in the white house by the apple orchard. All her life Mrs. Tillby had tended the trees and picked and sold apples. All her life Mrs. Tillby wondered how it would be to live someplace else.

One morning Mrs. Tillby woke up and went downstairs. Her son Wes was fixing breakfast.

"Wes," said Mrs. Tillby. "All my life I've lived in this house, watching the orchard change with the seasons. All my life I've wondered how it would be to live someplace else, and now is the time for me to try. So tomorrow I'm leaving to visit your brother Les in the big city. If it suits me, I'll stay."

"But. . . Mother!" said Wes. "This house has always been your home. Where else would you want to live?"

"I don't know, dear," said Mrs. Tillby. "I just know that I want to try living someplace else."

The next day Mrs. Tillby put her suitcase in the back of the old green truck. She hugged Wes good-bye. Then Mrs. Tillby drove off down the road.

The country road that wound around the apple orchard became a six-lane highway. Cars and trucks rushed by. Houses gave way to tall buildings.

Mrs. Tillby pulled up in front of Les's apartment house. It was forty stories high. Les was waiting for her, looking handsome in his gray banker's suit.

"Welcome to the city, Mother!" said Les, kissing her on the top of her head. "I know you're going to love it here!"

"Thank you, dear," said Mrs. Tillby. She stood on tiptoe to reach his cheek. "It looks that way to me!"

Mrs. Tillby was happy in the city. She went to museums and theaters and stores and restaurants. She saw all sorts of people and tried all kinds of food. At night, from her bedroom window, she could see the lights of the city shining brighter than the stars.

But after a few weeks she wanted to move on.

"I can see why you love city life, Les," said Mrs. Tillby, "with all the hustle and bustle, and so much to see and do. But it doesn't feel like home to me, so I want to try living someplace else."

"Oh, Mother," said Les, "stay a while longer. You haven't seen half of the city."

Mrs. Tillby patted Les's hand.

"You're a dear boy," she said, "and a lovely host. But tomorrow I'm leaving to visit your sister Tess at the seashore. If it suits me, I'll stay."

The next day Mrs. Tillby put her suitcase in the back of the old green truck. She hugged Les good-bye and set off toward the highway.

Soon the six-lane highway thinned out. The tall buildings gave way to houses again. Seagulls swooped and called overhead. Mrs. Tillby smelled salt in the air.

Mrs. Tillby pulled up to Tess's house. It stood on stilts at the edge of the ocean. Tess was waiting for her, wearing a fisherman's yellow slicker. The twins were waiting, too.

"Grandma! Grandma!" they cried.

"Welcome to the seashore, Mother!" said Tess. "You'll just love it here!"

"Thank you, dear," said Mrs. Tillby, hugging everyone at once. "I'm sure I will."

Mrs. Tillby did like the house on stilts. From her window she could see far out over the ocean. She spent hours gathering shells with the twins and helped Tess cook fresh fish and chowder for dinner. Every evening Mrs. Tillby went for a barefoot walk along the shore. At night the sound of the waves lulled her to sleep.

But after a few weeks she needed to move on.

"I understand why you love living by the shore, Tess," said Mrs. Tillby. "The sea is always changing, and the air is ever so clear. But it doesn't feel like home to me, so I want to try living someplace else."

"Oh, Mother," said Tess, "you haven't been here long enough. Wait until you see the wild waves at neap tide!"

Mrs. Tillby patted her hand.

"You're a dear girl," she said, "and you've made me very welcome. But tomorrow I'm leaving to visit your brother Jackson in the mountains. If it suits me, I'll stay."

The next day Mrs. Tillby hugged Tess and the twins. She put her suitcase in the back of the old green truck and drove off down the road.

The road narrowed and became twisty. Sand dunes gave way to hills, and hills to mountains. Hawks wheeled above her.

Mrs. Tillby pulled up to Jackson's house. It was made of stone and sat on the edge of a cliff. Jackson came out to greet her in his thick woolen lumberjacket. He wrapped his mother in a big bear hug.

"Welcome to the mountains, Mother!" he said. "You're going to love it here!"

"Thank you, dear," said Mrs. Tillby, adjusting her glasses. "I can't imagine anything nicer."

Mrs. Tillby loved the mountains and the smell of pine that filled the air.
Every night she lit a fire in the great stone fireplace. Winter came, and snow
fell like a thick white blanket. Jackson's wife taught her how to ski.

But after a few weeks she felt like moving on.

"I know why you love the mountains, Jackson," said Mrs. Tillby. "You
can see for miles around, and there is more wildlife than I ever dreamed of.
But it just doesn't feel like home to me. I'm going to try someplace else."

"Oh, Mother," said Jackson, "at least stay the winter. And you must see
the mountains in early spring."

Mrs. Tillby patted his hand.

"You're a dear boy," she said, "and you've treated me like a guest. But I
am leaving tomorrow."

"But Mother Tillby," said Jackson's wife, whose name was Bess. "Where
will you go? You're tired of the orchard, you've tried the mountains and the
seashore, and big-city life doesn't suit you. What is left?"

"I don't know, dear," said Mrs. Tillby. "There must be someplace else."

The next day Mrs. Tillby put her suitcase in the back of the old green truck. She hugged Jackson and his wife, and drove down the mountain road.

Mrs. Tillby tried living in lots of places. She stayed in a cabin by a lake and in a fire tower high above a forest. She stayed in an adobe hut in the middle of the desert. She even spent time on a riverboat!

But everywhere she went, it was the same. Mrs. Tillby was always happy at first. After a few weeks she always wanted to move on.

One morning Mrs. Tillby put her suitcase in the back of the old green truck for the last time. Wearily she set off back toward the apple orchard.

"All my life," said Mrs. Tillby as she drove, "I've wanted to live someplace else. Now I've tried all kinds of places, and nothing suits me."

Mrs. Tillby had almost reached the road that led to the orchard when she came to a crossroads. There, parked at a gas station, she saw a shiny silver trailer. FOR SALE read the sign in the window. Mrs. Tillby leaped out of the old green truck. She asked to see the inside of the trailer.

The silver trailer had a cozy bedroom, a tiny bathroom, and a kitchen that folded out of sight.

Mrs. Tillby bought it on the spot.

Now, every few weeks, Mrs. Tillby sets off in the old green truck with the shiny silver trailer attached behind. Sometimes she visits Les in the city, or Tess at the seashore, or Jackson and his wife in the mountains. Sometimes she stays in other places. And in the autumn Mrs. Tillby goes back to the white house by the orchard to help Wes pick and sell apples.

Mrs. Tillby is always home, and she is always someplace else.

P